What Kids Say About
Carole Marsh Mysteries . . .

I love the real locations! Reading the book always makes me want to go and visit them all on our next family vacation. My Mom says maybe, but I can't wait!

One day, I want to be a real kid in one of Ms. Marsh's mystery books. I think it would be fun, and I think I am a real character anyway. I filled out the application and sent it in. I hope they pick me!

History was not my favorite subject till I started reading Carole Marsh Mysteries. Ms. Marsh really brings history to life. Also, she leaves room for the scary and fun.

I think the characters are so smart and brave. They are lucky because they get to do so much cool stuff! I always wish I could be right there with them!

The kids in the story are cool and funny! They make me laugh a lot! I like that there are boys and girls in the story of different ages. Some mysteries I outgrow, but I can always find a favorite character to identify with in these books.

They are scary, but not too scary. They are funny. I learn a lot. There is always food, which makes me hungry. I feel like I am there.

What Parents and Teachers Say About Carole Marsh Mysteries . . .

I think kids love these books because they have such a wealth of detail. I know I learn a lot reading them! It's an engaging way to look at the history of any place or event. I always say I'm only going to read one chapter to the kids, but that never happens—it's always two or three, at least!
—Librarian

Reading the mystery and going on the field trip—Scavenger Hunt in hand—was the most fun our class ever had! It really brought the place and its history to life. They loved the real kids characters and all the humor. I loved seeing them learn that reading is an experience to enjoy!
—4th grade teacher

Carole Marsh is really on to something with these unique mysteries. They are so clever; kids want to read them all. The Teacher's Guides are chock full of activities, recipes, and additional fascinating information. My kids thought I was an expert on the subject—and with this tool, I felt like it!
—3rd grade teacher

My students loved writing their own mystery book! Ms. Marsh's reproducible guidelines are a real jewel. They learned about copyright and more & ended up with their own book they were so proud of!
—Reading/Writing Teacher

"The kids seem very realistic—my children seemed to relate to the characters. Also, it is educational by expanding their knowledge about the famous places in the books."

"They are what children like: mysteries and adventures with children they can relate to."

"Encourages reading for pleasure."

"This series is great. It can be used for reluctant readers, and as a history supplement."

CAROLE MARSH MYSTERIES

Dear Alien:

The Little Green Man Mystery

By Carole Marsh

Carole Marsh Mysteries™ and its skull colophon are the property
of Carole Marsh and Gallopade International.

Published by Gallopade International/Carole Marsh Books. Printed
in the United States of America.

Managing Editor: Sherry Moss
Senior Editor: Janice Baker
Assistant Editor: Mike Kelly
Cover Design and Illustrations: Yvonne Ford

Gallopade International is introducing SAT words that kids
need to know in each new book tht we publish. The SAT words
are bold in the story. Look for this special logo beside each word.

Gallopade is proud to be a member and supporter of these
educational organizations and associations:

American Library Association
American Booksellers Association
International Reading Association
National Association for Gifted Children
The National School Supply and Equipment Association
The National Council for the Social Studies
Museum Store Association
Association of Partners for Public Lands

20 Years Ago . . .

As a mother and an author, one of the fondest periods of my life was when I decided to write mystery books for children. At this time (1979) kids were pretty much glued to the TV, something parents and teachers complained about the way they do about web surfing and blogging today.

I decided to set each mystery in a real place—a place kids could go and visit for themselves after reading the book. And I also used real children as characters. Usually a couple of my own children served as characters, and I had no trouble recruiting kids from the book's location to also be characters.

Also, I wanted all the kids—boys and girls of all ages—to participate in solving the mystery. And, I wanted kids to learn something as they read. Something about the history of the location. And I wanted the stories to be funny. That formula of real+scary+smart+fun served me well.

I love getting letters from teachers and parents who say they read the book with their class or child, then visited the historic site and saw all the places in the mystery for themselves. What's so great about that? What's great is that you and your children have an experience that bonds you together forever. Something you shared. Something you both cared about at the time. Something that crossed all age levels—a good story, a good scare, a good laugh!

20 years later,

Carole Marsh

Christina "Mystery Girl" Mimi Papa Grant

Hey, kids! As you see, here we are ready to embark on another of our exciting Carole Marsh Mystery adventures. My grandchildren often travel with me all over the world as I research new books. We have a great time together, and learn things we will carry with us for the rest of our lives!

I hope you will go to www.carolemarshmysteries.com and explore the many Carole Marsh Mysteries series!

Well, the Mystery Girl is all tuned up and ready for "take-off!" Gotta go...Papa says so! Wonder what I've forgotten this time?

Happy "Armchair Travel" Reading,

Mimi

P.S. Send me a postcard ... and receive a postcard from an ... ALIEN!

About the Characters

Paul Post is the postmaster of the post office in Postcard, Pennsylvania. He's quiet, soft-spoken and a bit of a worrywart. He's not a whiz at electronics, but can hold his own. He hates to drive, and doesn't always like to be the one in charge.

Penelope Post is a street-smart, independent mother with her own postcard company. She doesn't know much about technology, and likes to run around in curlers and sweat clothes. She loves homeschooling her children and taking trips, because every trip is an education you can't get in books.

Peter Post inherited his mother's love for traveling. He's an 11-year-old who loves to figure out puzzles, riddles, and a good mystery, of course. Peter never goes anywhere without his backpack, which contains his laptop and spy paraphernalia.

Piper Post inherited her mother's sassiness. She's a very smart 10-year-old, but doesn't like school very much. Piper loves her adventures with her brother and usually uncovers the last bit of information to help Peter solve the mystery. She also loves to tell knock-knock jokes, just to annoy Peter!

Books in This Series

#1 Dear Alien: The Little Green Man Mystery

#2 Dear Bats: The Creepy Cave Caper Mystery

#3 Dear Pirate: The Buried Treasure Mystery

Hey Kids,
Don't forget to send Carole Marsh
a postcard—and get one back . . .
from an ALIEN!

Table of Contents

Prologue

Travel with the Post Family:

Colorado Springs, Colorado

Postcard, Pennsylvania

Area 51

Dayton, Ohio

Roswell, New Mexico

In Search of Aliens

Prologue

Peter Post sprang out of bed and rubbed his eyes with the palms of his hands. A second later, he realized the music flying around inside his head was coming from the iPod clipped to his boxers. The sun radiating through the window hadn't woken Peter. The aroma of Swedish pancakes coming from the kitchen had invaded his nostrils. He didn't like Swedish pancakes, but his mom did. If she was making them, it meant only one thing.

He snatched his shirt and pants off the chair and stumbled over a pile of clothes. When his right foot landed on his football, he surfed across the room, right past his new poster of a blond James Bond and his old poster of Albert Einstein. He fell into his desk, knocking over his alarm clock and a convoy of Hot Wheels cars. He caught the clock a second before it crashed to the floor. The Hot Wheels landed safely on another pile of clothes near the desk.

Peter yanked on his jeans and t-shirt and scooped his worn pair of Nikes off the floor. Peter was tall for his age and had inherited his dad's curious boyish nature, too. But his dark hair and mischievous sky-blue eyes came from his mom. This morning his hair poked out in different directions like a character from an episode of Pokémon.

As he left the room, he tapped the doorpost with his hand and noticed the Post-It note his younger sister, Piper, had left. It read, *Breakfast at eight, it's your fate, so don't be late.*

As Peter rushed down the stairs, he hopped on one foot, and then the other, pulling on his shoes. He pitched over and fell the last couple of stairs, landing on his feet like a cat. He ran into the kitchen and froze. Piper sat at the table digging into a large bowl of Post Toasties. There was a plate of half-eaten Swedish pancakes on the table, but his mom wasn't there.

"Tell me I'm not late?" he begged Piper.

Suddenly, their mother walked out of the pantry with a bag of powdered sugar. She was wearing her usual baggy black sweats. One of the pink foam curlers in her jet-black hair hung by a few strands.

"Ready for a short road trip, Peter?" she asked.

The Race

"Can too!" Piper said, as her mom, Penelope Post, pulled their large SUV into the closest parking space at the only post office in Postcard, Pennsylvania.

"No you can't," Peter shot back.

Mom glanced in the rearview mirror at her children.

"Okay, I'll just have to show you." Piper pursed her lips.

"Fine, but don't come crying to me when you lose," Peter said.

Mom smiled. Peter and Piper's **camaraderie** was infectious. It was the same routine every few weeks when they went to the post office to drop off her shipment of designer postcards. The race to the front door was on. Piper would challenge and Peter would accept. And it was Mom's job to say, "Go!"

Peter and Piper eyeballed each other like two gunslingers ready to shoot it out. They sat on the edge of their seats, ready to bolt as soon as she gave the word.

Mom pulled down the sun visor and looked in the mirror to straighten out the scarf covering her curlers. A Post-It note, stuck to the mirror, reminded her to pick up the extra school supplies she used to homeschool Peter and Piper.

She spotted her husband, Paul Post, through the building's front window. He was stamping packages and tossing them into a roll-around bin that had the word MAIL printed in big letters on all sides. Paul was the town's postmaster. Until he had recently hired Jamie Haldeman, he had been Postcard's only postman for over five years.

"GO!" she shouted.

Like a flash, the van's side doors flew open and they were off. Peter and Piper bolted like two racehorses from their starting posts. They made it to the curb at the same time. Peter bounded over the curb onto the grass and slid wildly for a few feet, losing precious time. Piper dashed past him and tagged the door's shiny aluminum handle.

"I won! I won!" she squealed.

"You got lucky." Peter tried to hide his smile.

"No, I didn't. You let me win like you always do." Piper flung the door open and ran inside.

Mom opened the back door of the van just as Peter appeared at her side to help carry the boxes of postcards inside. Internet sales had been good for the postcard company she'd started when Peter was just three years old.

"You know, one day she's going to beat you fair and square," Mom said.

"Yeah, maybe. But when she does, she'll always wonder if she really won or if I let her win," he said with a smile. The two boxes he carried were covered in Post-It notes with addresses written on them. He opened the post office door for his mom with his free hand.

"You're a mischievous child," she said.

Piper had disappeared into the bowels of the building to find her dad, who wasn't out front anymore. Peter set the packages on the counter and strolled over to the posting board, which had personal ads, lost and found notices, and church gatherings posted on it. It even held job postings from several businesses in town. Reading it kept him in touch with the goings-on of this tiny metropolis.

Piper suddenly appeared with her arms wrapped around her dad's waist. Although Piper was only one year younger than Peter, she was almost a head shorter. She had somehow ended up with hazel eyes, but had inherited her mom's dark hair, which she usually wore in pigtails. The joy of life, reflected in her freckled face, delighted everyone she came in contact with.

"Can Peter and I go look at some mail, Dad?" Piper begged.

"Sure, you two go ahead," he said. "Just don't cause any problems back there. I'll help your mom."

"We'll be good, Dad, don't worry." Peter hurried to catch up with his sister. She was already yakking with Jamie Haldeman. Jamie was sorting mail into mailbox slots.

"Can we, can we? I love looking through the dead letter file," Piper pleaded.

"You sure can," Jamie said. "Just make sure you put back what you pull out. Since there's no readable address on them, we have to ship them off to Philly this afternoon."

"What for?" Peter asked.

"They open the letters and try to find addresses they can return or forward them to," Jamie said. "If there are no addresses, they hold onto the letters for two years. If no one files a claim by then, they burn them."

Piper shrieked. "Oh my gosh! Oh my gosh! Peter, come here! Hurry up! I found a postcard sent by *little green aliens!*"

Little Green Aliens

Piper stood near a white plastic box marked USPS. A sign on the box read Dead Letters Only. She handed Peter the postcard. The front half of the postcard had a picture of little green space aliens, the other half had the To and From addresses.

The card was really beat up. It must have gotten rained on, Peter thought.

Almost all of the writing on the address side of the postcard was smeared and unreadable. The back of the card wasn't much better. Peter had trouble reading it.

He held the card up to a light. "From the postmark stamps, it looks like it's bounced through several post offices," Peter said. "It was mailed less than a week ago. Look at how tiny the writing is. Whoever wrote this writes smaller than Mom does. I think it says:

Dear Alien,

... life here is lonely. I miss our home. ... on this planet ... I don't ... people look at me funny ... I am wearing my favorite green ... It has ... plates and does ... cover ... skin ... I guess the young scare them. Only ... understand. In ... to take control of ... I must blend in ... I ... school ... I do not know ... Meet me at the OSETIUFOMRC next Saturday night.

Your Yellow Alien

Dear Alien, Life here is lonely. I miss our home...planet. People look at me funny...my green...skin...scare them...to take control...I must blend in...Meet me at the OSETIUFOMRC next Saturday night. It's signed: Lonely Alien."

"I'm confused, what does OSETIUFOMRC stand for?" Piper asked.

"SETI is an acronym for Search for Extraterrestrial Intelligence and UFO is Unidentified Flying Object," Peter said.

"How do you know that?" Piper was always amazed at how much her brother knew.

"I saw a program about it on the Discovery Channel," Peter said. "I'm not sure what the O stands for or the MRC."

"Maybe the O stands for ought," Piper said.

"Ought?" Peter asked. Piper had always **perplexed** him with her crazy logic. He used to try to figure it out, but had learned to just go with the flow.

"You know," Piper began, "like in 'we Ought not be Searching for Extraterrestrial Intelligence,' especially ugly, little green men. The last thing we need is for some scary aliens to find out where we live and make us their zombie slaves. I don't want to be anyone's slave," she squealed, waving her hands wildly in the air. "And most certainly not a zombie slave."

Girls, Peter thought. I hope it gets easier to understand them as I get older. "Okaaayyyyy." A big smile crossed Peter's face as he looked back and forth between Piper and the postcard a few times. "OSETI, UFOs, and a lonely alien. My lady, methinks a mystery is afoot!" Peter said in his best Sherlock Holmes voice.

"Oh great! Here we go again." Piper threw her hands in the air. "How can a mystery be afoot? A foot is a foot, not a mystery. That is, unless you have Dad's huge feet!"

Electromagnetic What?

Mom stood by the gas pump as their SUV chugged down gallon after gallon of gas. Attached to the trailer hitch was Breadloaf, the name Piper had given their bread-loaf shaped, 1968, 26-foot, silver Airstream Overlander trailer. It had transported them on many of their adventures. Although it was their command post, she had to admit it had seen better days. It was battered and beaten, but Peter loved to keep its silver exterior polished and gleaming.

Peter was clacking away on his laptop computer when Piper came out of Breadloaf with tinfoil wrapped around her head. Her trademark pigtails poked out of a hole on each side. There were also two holes for her eyes and a slit for her mouth. The two silver antennae protruding upward from the top of her head added the finishing touch.

"Come on, James Bond. Where are we heading?" Piper asked.

"The name is Post, Peter Post," Peter said, using a British accent, "and I'm checking out the information on the copy of the postcard we made as we speak." Peter didn't look up from the computer. "But wherever we're heading, we need to be there this Saturday."

"Why's that, Alien Hunter?" Piper asked, hoping her brother would look up.

Peter's keyboard clacking continued. "Because, the postcard alien told the other alien to meet her at the OSETIUFOMRC on Saturday."

"Why do you think it's a *her*?" Piper said, forgetting about her alien disguise for a moment.

"I don't know," Peter said. "I guess her writing sounds like a girl. But maybe her species doesn't have boys or girls. Maybe they only have *its*." Peter looked up from the computer and saw his sister, just as his mom took their picture.

Peter shook his head. "See, I was right. They are only its."

"Watch what you say, earthling, or I'll zap you with my antennae," Piper said, pointing one of her antennae toward her brother.

Mom pulled the picture out of the old Polaroid camera and waved it in the air. "Here we have the Alien Hunter and his faithful alien sidekick, Silver Streak."

"Let me see! Let me see!" Piper squawked, trying to grab it from her mom's hands.

Peter tried to ignore his crazy sister. "What did you tell Dad?"

Mom handed the Polaroid to her daughter. "I told him that this SETI thing sounded like an education just waiting to happen. And that you guys really wanted to learn about the search for extra...terres...oh, you know I can never say that word."

"What did he say about that?" Peter giggled.

"Oh, the usual when I ask him if we can go galloping off." Mom deepened her voice like Paul's. "Are you sure you're going to be okay?" she boomed. "He's such a worrywart."

"I wish he could come with us," Piper said.

"He wanted to," her mom said, "but he's saving his vacation time for our big summer trip to Kentucky." She gave Piper a big "it's okay" hug. "Besides, with us out of his hair he can get something done on his post-graduate work.

"Speaking of schoolwork," Mom said, "This trip is a great idea and a chance for you to learn some science. So, I'll expect an essay on this SETI thing, and anything else you learn on this trip, from each of you after you solve this mystery." Mom pushed a loose curler back in place.

"I knew this was going to happen!" Piper said. "I was hoping to make it through one trip without having to write a dumb old essay."

"Maybe next trip," Mom said.

"I found it!" Peter declared, turning the laptop so his mom could see.

"Found what?" Mom asked.

"I found what the O in OSETI is, and it's not *ought*." Peter made a face at his alien sister. "It stands for Optical Search for Extraterrestrial Intelligence. There's a large SETI observatory in Colorado Springs, run by a Dr. Huxley. That's where we need to start our investigation."

"What in this world is Optical—?" Mom started to ask.

"It's not *in this world,* Mom, it's *out of this world,*" Piper interrupted, jiggling her alien-looking head.

Peter continued, "It has something to do with laser pulses and a portion of the electromagnetic spectrum. This Dr. Huxley believes that any alien life in the universe would use lasers to communicate with us, not radio signals."

Mom shook her head. "You lost me at electro...mayonnaise or whatever." The gas pump stopped and Mom put the hose back in its cradle and capped the tank.

"It's easy, Mom," Peter said. "The SETI program officially started back in the early 1960s. But up until recently, scientists have only *listened* for radio signals from outer space. Now they're *searching* space for lasers that might contain messages from other intelligent life in the universe."

"Intelligent? Then why talk to us?" Piper said. "We'll just **foil** their plans and shoot them out of the sky when they come to make us into zombie slaves by stealing our brains. That is unless they've already snuck in the backdoor, like our postcard friend or all those politicians in Washington. Dad's always saying that somebody must have stolen their brains."

"You won't have to wait for them!" Peter said. "I'm going to make you my alien zombie slave—right now!" He leaped up and chased his sister around the SUV.

"The earthlings are attacking! Run for your lives!" Piper shrieked as she ran, waving her arms wildly.

Mom removed her printed gas receipt from the pump. "I swear this thing gulps down more gas every time I fill up. Well, I guess we're off to Colorado Springs, Colorado then. Post-haste!"

The Maze

Like his favorite spy, James Bond, Peter scoped out the maze of buildings in front of him as he wiggled his way through an opening in the chain link gate. While he waited for Piper to do the same, he scanned several of the buildings. Most were brick or metal. Some looked like old office buildings, others were like airplane hangars. That is where we'll start, he thought, as he began to weave his way through the maze at Wright-Patterson Air Force Base in Dayton, Ohio.

"Are you sure we should be doing this?" Piper asked. "This is a military post. We're probably not supposed to be here."

"I think it's closed down," Peter replied. "The guard shack we passed was empty."

"We should have waited with Mom for the road service to come," Piper said.

"Hey, it was Mom's idea for us to go in search of food.   But thinking about it, if anything happens to us, it'll be all your fault," Peter teased.

"No it won't!" Piper shrieked.

"Yes, it will. If you hadn't told Mom you were hungry, she wouldn't have gotten off the highway and Breadloaf wouldn't have blown a tire."

"Okay, so that part was me," Piper replied. "But you're the one dragging us through this maze of buildings."

"You're right," Peter said. "I am, but I just gave you a *post-hoc* argument."

Piper shook her head. "Okay, I'll bite. What does *post-hoc* mean?"

"It's the mistake of arguing that since one thing happened before another thing, the first thing caused the second thing," Peter said, smiling.

"Now you're starting to sound like me," Piper said. "Where did you get that from, PBS?"

"It's very educational, you know!" Peter said.

Peter pointed at the door of a building that appeared to be an airplane hangar. "If this air base isn't closed," he said, "we could look for the Post Exchange, but I don't think they'd let us inside. Maybe we'll get lucky and find some snack machines in here."

As Peter reached for the door handle, a bald-headed man emerged from between two buildings across the street. "STOP!" he shouted.

Peter's mom had always told him that he had a good eye for judging people, and right now he didn't like the way this guy was glaring at them.

"Sorry, sir," Peter called out. "Our mom told us we're not allowed to talk to strangers."

Peter flung the door open and hauled Piper through the opening. He let the door slam shut behind them. It was dark inside with only a few ceiling lights turned on. It didn't look like an active hangar; there were no airplanes, just huge crates, machinery, and big orange metal drums lining the walls. Peter, with Piper in tow, ran across the back of the hangar and dove behind some of the drums.

"Hmmm! I don't see any snack machines," Piper grumbled.

"Don't worry," Peter said. "After we ditch this guy, I'll find you some snack machines."

"What's for-mal-di-hide?" Piper whispered.

Peter peeked over his shoulder at his sister, like she was nuts. "What are you talking about?"

"This stuff," Piper said, pointing at the word FORMALDEHYDE on one of the barrels.

"Oh!" Peter said. "It's a chemical used to preserve bodies or organs."

"Yuck! How do you know that?" Piper asked.

"Come on, sis!" Peter said. "I'm training to be a spy, remember? Good spies know everything." The outside door opened. "Duck down!" Peter ordered his sister.

"I know you kids are hiding in here!" Baldy shouted. "You're not supposed to be on government property without a military escort. If you don't come out, I'll get the Military Police to find you. Now show yourselves!" he demanded.

Peter saw a partially opened door about five feet from where he and Piper knelt. He put his forefinger up to his lips and nodded to her to follow. They quietly scooted through the doorway to a set of stairs.

The stairs had no lights. Only the dim light from the hangar lit their way. After descending the first flight, Peter tried the door. It was locked. There was a lighted keypad next to it.

"Let's try the next level," Piper whispered.

As they reached the next landing, Piper nearly screamed. She had walked into a massive spider web. She jumped up and down, trying to wipe the sticky web out of her hair.

"Calm down," Peter whispered, helping her pull the web off.

They tried two more doors with no success. Oh my gosh! Oh my gosh! This is really getting creepy, Piper thought. A drop of icy liquid dripped onto her neck and ran down her spine. She shivered as she swiped at the moisture with her hand. A second later, she stepped into something gooey and almost slipped. It smelled like blood. The dampness seeped into her bones, as goose bumps took up temporary residence on her arms and the back of her neck.

The last floor was in total darkness except for the light emitted by the door's keypad. Peter tried to open it. The door hadn't closed all the way, so the electronic latch hadn't locked it. It suddenly dawned on Peter that if this military post was closed, why did they electronically lock doors? Plus, he'd never heard of an aircraft hangar with basement levels below it.

"Oops!" Peter thought.

Peter opened the door slowly. He was afraid it was going to squeak. It moved without a sound. After entering the pitch-black room, he quietly shut the door. He suddenly remembered the flashlight tucked into a pocket on the side of his backpack. Like his iPod, he never went anywhere without it. He grabbed it and flicked the switch. Light flooded the room.

"We could've used that coming down the stairs, Mr. Spy!" Piper grumbled. She let go of Peter's arm, which she had been holding onto like her life depended on it. "Peter, what if Baldy gets the MPs?"

"He won't," Peter said. "He didn't have an ID badge, so I doubt he even works here."

"So then why is he chasing us?" Piper asked.

Peter spoke in his James Bond voice. "That, my dear, is the question! *Isn't it?*"

Alien Autopsies

Peter shifted the beam of light around the room. The room looked like an old morgue, and was similar to the ones he had seen on forensic television shows, just not as modern.

When Piper realized where they were, she grabbed Peter's arm again and squeezed it tightly. "Is this what I think it is?" she whispered.

"Yeah! I wonder how many post-mortem exams they did down here," Peter said. "I've never heard of a morgue in an aircraft hangar; they're usually in hospitals." With Piper holding on tightly, Peter stepped toward the three stainless steel tables in the center of the room. The flashlight's beam reflected off of something green.

Peter dragged Piper with him over to the table and bent down to take a whiff and a closer look. Something had dried to a hard green glaze with no real odor. He didn't know what it was, but he didn't think formaldehyde was green.

Peter heard footsteps on the stairs outside the door. He pushed Piper through another door beyond the tables near some metal sinks. Just as they slipped through the door, the flashlight's beam settled on an emergency exit sign. It showed the layout of the rooms on this level and their exits. But what really caught his eye was the lettering at the top of the sign:

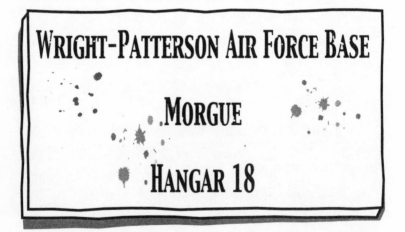

WRIGHT-PATTERSON AIR FORCE BASE

MORGUE

HANGAR 18

It didn't happen often, but for a few seconds Peter was speechless. The image of him, his dad, and his sister sitting in front of the TV watching a movie about an alien spacecraft crashing in Roswell, New Mexico flooded his mind as he shut off his flashlight.

"Did you see that sign, Peter?" Piper whispered. "Do you remember that movie we watched with Dad last summer? It was called *Hangar 18* and was about alien autopsies done at Wright-Patterson in the late 1940s and early 1950s. I knew I'd heard of this military post before!"

"Shhh!" Peter whispered. A beam of light flashed around the morgue. Peter peeked through the slightly opened door. Baldy was shining a flashlight through the small window on the locked door. Unless he knew the code, there was no way for him to open it.

The light in the lab disappeared. Peter remained still until Baldy's footsteps faded into the distance. When he was sure Baldy was gone, he turned on his own flashlight again.

Peter and Piper were in a long, narrow room. The musty air had a hint of a medicinal odor, like being in a hospital. A row of stainless steel, coffin-shaped metal containers was perched along the wall. Their once shiny exteriors had faded away with time. Each container was about four feet long with a curved, rusty-hinged lid. He counted 11 of them. The containers were connected to valves on the back wall by two metal braided hoses. Words printed on the wall above the valves said *Liquid Nitrogen* and *Liquid Oxygen*. Names were scrawled on the end of each container:

"You're not thinking what I'm thinking?" Piper asked.

"Probably," Peter replied. "Let's find out." Peter stepped toward Smiley's container. He unlatched the hooks that held the lid secure.

SQUUUEEEEKK!

As Peter raised the lid, the high-pitched noise pierced the silence, jolting Piper. He half expected smoky, frigid air to come rushing out, but nothing did. There was nothing inside except the same hard, glazed, green goop like that on the autopsy table.

"Empty," Peter said, relieved. He lowered the lid and noticed a small yellowish piece of paper on the floor. He scooped it up. The paper was old. It also had a dried green stain on it, along with shoeprints. The message on it had been typed on an old typewriter, not a computer, except for the signature at the bottom, which had long ago faded away. He handed the paper to Piper.

Piper read it out loud.

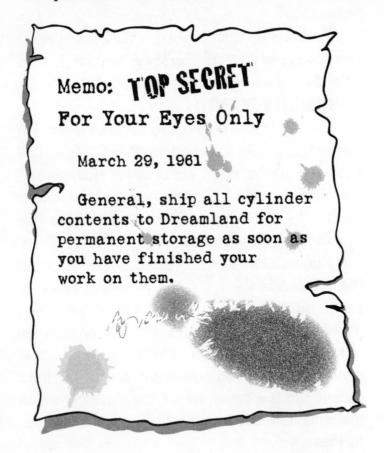

Memo: **TOP SECRET**
For Your Eyes Only

March 29, 1961

General, ship all cylinder
contents to Dreamland for
permanent storage as soon as
you have finished your
work on them.

Peter and Piper looked at each other. *What
had they stumbled across?*

Pepsi Please

Peter guided Piper down several hallways to a staircase on the other side of the hangar. The door unlocked with a push bar from the inside. They tiptoed up the four flights of stairs.

The kids entered the hangar behind the huge wooden crates they had seen earlier. There was an exit only twenty feet away. Peter's eyes scoured the hangar to make sure Baldy wasn't around, then he ran to the door. He waited a second before waving for Piper to follow. He opened the outside door just a crack. No one was there.

Peter and Piper emerged from the hangar into bright sunlight. They squinted their eyes as they weaved their way around some large air conditioning units and air vents toward the front of the structure.

GROOWWLL!

"Did you hear that? I'm really hungry, Peter!" Piper said, rubbing her tummy.

"I know, I'm doing my best to..." Piper plowed into Peter when he halted suddenly.

They had stumbled upon a covered patio with several snack and drink machines. There was also an area set aside with several ashtrays and signs saying, *Smoking Allowed*. There was no one there at the moment.

"Voila! I told you I'd find you some snack machines," Peter said, walking over to the drink machine. He stuffed quarters into the rusty change slot as fast as it would swallow them and pressed the Pepsi button. "Man, all this sneaking around has made me thirsty."

"You're not as thirsty as I am hungry," Piper replied. "I could eat a horse, if I ate horses, which I don't, so I guess I can't eat a horse. Okay, I can eat a cow!"

Peter peeked around the corner to the front of the hangar. Suddenly, his body stiffened. Baldy was leaning against an Air Force blue SUV. He was in handcuffs. Two military policemen

questioning him were dressed in camouflage
fatigues with thick, black MP armbands. One of
the MPs mumbled something into his radio, while
the other shoved Baldy in the back of the SUV.

This definitely wasn't a good idea, no matter
how hungry Piper is, Peter thought.

The SUV screeched off.

"Piper, I don't care what you eat," Peter
said. "Just hurry up and get what you want
before someone wants to smoke and comes out
here. Oh, don't forget to get Mom a Pepsi and
some chips."

"I already did," Piper said. Her arms were
loaded down with snacks. "Let's go, I'm tired of
sneaking around. Besides, you're causing me to
develop post-traumatic stress syndrome. See, I
watch PBS sometimes, too!"

Peter led the way back through the maze of
buildings to the fence. As they wiggled through
the gate again, Peter spied a tow truck pulling
away. That meant the tire on their SUV had been
fixed! Breadloaf's door was open. Their mom
was sitting in front of the TV in a post-hypnotic
state watching one of her favorite soap operas.

"Oh! There you guys are," Mom said, coming
out of her trance. She reached up and tucked

another loose curler back up under her scarf. "I was beginning to wonder what was taking you so long. Did you bring me a Pepsi? I'm dying of thirst."

They were back on the road in no time. After scarfing down some chips, Peter whipped out his mom's laptop. He needed to figure out *where* Dreamland was. He was already sure he knew *what* it was!

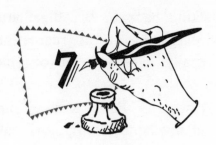

Solving Mysteries 101

The sun, set in a brilliant blue sky, sparkled off the red sandstone rock cliffs and immense boulders that jutted skyward above the bright green trees in the Garden of the Gods in Colorado Springs, Colorado. This park has to be one of the most amazing parks on earth, Peter thought. He loved to travel and this was one of the nicer RV parks they had seen. The park had all the things they needed, plus a pool, miniature golf course, and a recreation building with video games, ping-pong, and pool tables.

"Peter, do you think we can figure out who sent that postage-paid postcard?" Piper asked while walking back to Breadloaf after a lively game of ping-pong at the recreation building. "There really aren't a lot of clues in the message."

"Don't worry," Peter said. "Between our brains and my laptop computer, we'll find out who the alien is. You know, a mystery is like a puzzle. First, you locate the pieces that make sense, then you put those together and they will lead you to the next piece. The hardest thing to remember is to focus on the whole puzzle and not one piece."

"Okay," Piper said. "But the postcard was in such bad shape we couldn't even read a return address. It could have come from anywhere and there's a lot of anywhere out there from sea to shining sea."

"Not exactly, while you were napping..." Peter said.

"Excuusse me!" Piper said. "I'm a growing child. I need my beauty sleep to keep this face cute. Plus, sleep helps to develop my brain. That way if the aliens take it, at least they'll be getting a smart one. Speaking of aliens, do you think that bald guy back in Dayton could have been an alien in human disguise?"

Peter ignored Piper's outburst. "I went back and looked at the photocopy we made of the postcard. I could make out three numbers on the return zip code," he said. "The first, fourth, and fifth numbers, an 8, a 0, and a 1. I went on the Internet earlier and found that they match the zip codes of several towns in New Mexico, Arizona, and Nevada."

"New Mexico!" Piper said. "Would Roswell be one of them?"

"Yep, and one in Nevada is for a town called Alamo," Peter said. "It's just outside of Dreamland or as most people call it, Area 51, which is where we'll go tomorrow after we finish up with Dr. Huxley at the SETI observatory."

"What is Area 51, anyway?" Piper asked.

"It's a top secret aircraft and weapons test range," Peter said, "and some people think Unidentified Flying Objects—called UFOs—might be hidden there."

"Wow!" cried Piper. "I can't wait to get there! Let's go!"

When Piper entered Breadloaf, her mom was sitting at the table waving her hands in front of her face to dry her wet nail polish. "Hey guys! Did you have fun playing ping-pong?" she asked. Before they could answer, Mom flipped her hands around toward Piper. "Do you like this color? It's called Alien Green. I think it would look cute on you."

"I think I've had enough alien stuff, thank you," her daughter said. "Besides, right now, I think a big cheeseburger would look better in my hands. I'm starved. Let's unhook Breadloaf, which looks like our own alien flying saucer if you think about it, and go find a restaurant."

As he watched the SUV pull away from Breadloaf, Baldy stepped out from behind a wide tree. *Grinning, he pulled out his cell phone and dialed a familiar number.*

Galaxies Galore

It was a quick trip from the campground to Dr. Huxley's observatory.

"We're here," Mom called out. She whipped the SUV into the parking lot and rolled smoothly into a parking space. A sign greeted them by the front entrance to the building:

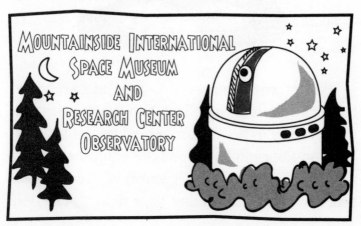

MOUNTAINSIDE INTERNATIONAL SPACE MUSEUM AND RESEARCH CENTER OBSERVATORY

The building stood in front of an ever-rising ridge of red sandstone boulders and cliffs. It had one of those astrological dome thing-a-ma-jigs for the telescope on it. There were also several large dish antennas off to the side of the building.

Piper buckled a small, pink fanny pack around her waist. Her mom had changed her curlers to blue ones and put on a new scarf and gray sweats before leaving the campground. "Mom, are you going to come with us or stay here?" Piper asked.

"I'm coming along," Mom replied, following Peter out of the SUV.

Peter was amazed at the ultra-modern building. It was split into two wings with the observatory in the center behind the lobby. The wing on the right contained the equipment room and labs where the recording and signal processing and analyzing was done. The left wing had offices and several large rooms filled with space paraphernalia.

The lobby was spacious. The walls held large, and in a few cases, very large, pictures of galaxies. There were spiral galaxies, elliptical galaxies, irregular galaxies, cluster galaxies, round galaxies, elongated sphere galaxies, and even flat galaxies. Several other families strolled around the lobby, peering at the incredibly detailed photos.

Mom ambled away from the photos and over to a young woman sitting behind a small information counter by the entrance to the observatory. "Hi, I'm Penelope Post, and my children are here to see Dr. Huxley," she said.

"Do they have an appointment?" the receptionist asked.

Peter spoke up. "Yes, we do."

"What are your names?" the receptionist asked with a smile.

"Peter and Piper Post," Peter said.

"Okay, hold on one minute," the receptionist said, as she picked up the phone handset and pressed a button on its base. "Dr. Huxley, Peter and Piper Post are here to see you." The receptionist nodded as she listened. "Yes, sir, I'll issue them passes and bring them to your office right away."

The receptionist handed Mom three passes.

"We only need two," Mom said. "I'll wait here for them. There's enough stuff here to keep me occupied until they get done."

The receptionist shrugged her shoulders, and escorted Peter and Piper down the hall to Dr. Huxley's office.

Listening for Aliens

Dr. Huxley liked his comfort. The sizable office held a beautiful wood desk, a leather couch and chairs, and several tables in the same cherry-colored wood as the desk. Stuck in a corner was a carpeted scratching post. The cat it belonged to was lurking behind the couch.

Dr. Huxley stood when Peter and Piper entered his office. "Hello, children," he said. "I'm Dr. Huxley and I understand you're interested in learning about optical SETI," he added, shaking their hands.

"Hello, Dr. Huxley," Peter said. "My name is Peter Post and this is my sister, Piper. We're writing essays about extraterrestrials. We're hoping you can provide us with information about optical and radio SETI."

"I'd be happy to," Huxley said. "Optical and radio SETI attack the problem of locating alien life from two different points of view, or maybe I should say, by using two different methods. I prefer the use of optical SETI because of KISS."

"You want to kiss an alien!" Piper said. "Don't you think that's carrying your work a little too far? I'm sure you love what you do, but trying to kiss an alien is strange. How would you do that, anyway?"

Huxley laughed. "No, no, Piper," he said. "KISS stands for Keep It Simple Stupid. In other words, don't make something more complicated than it is."

"Really," Piper said. "Can you teach Peter how to do that?"

"Just ignore her," Peter said. "She thinks she's the comedian in the family."

"Let's go to the observatory," Huxley suggested, leading Peter and Piper down a back hall toward the telescope.

"Here we go," Huxley said. "We use this 72-inch telescope to look for very short pulses of light that may come from nearby stars similar to our own sun. We also look at globular clusters and other galaxies outside of the Milky Way."

"Don't you get hungry with all these globular clusters and Milky Ways on your mind all the time?" Piper joked.

"My dear," Huxley said, faking a frown. "A globular cluster is a round collection of stars that orbits a galaxy's center, not a candy bar."

"Still sounds like a candy bar to me," Piper said, speaking like she was making a commercial. "A globular cluster is a smooth collection of chocolate and caramel that orbit the bar's chewy nugget center."

"What's so great about seeing a bunch of light pulses?" Peter asked, trying to get the conversation back on track.

Huxley pressed his fingertips together as he talked. "Many scientists believe making contact with alien life in the universe will rank as one of the most important events in human history," he explained.

"Okay, but how would green, ugly, big-headed aliens contact us?" Piper asked. "And once they're here, can they phone home?"

Huxley laughed. "One question at a time, dear," he said. "Until the last decade we believed alien contact would be through radio signals. One of the more popular radio SETI projects is Serendip, which searches for signals tuned to a frequency of 1420 megahertz." Huxley walked over to the telescope and flicked some switches to power it up.

"By frequency, he means radio stations, right?" Piper asked Peter in a whisper.

"Yeah, basically," Peter replied.

"Well," Piper said. "There are a bunch of radio frequencies where they can find aliens. You know, like those late-night talk radio stations Dad listens to. A lot of really strange people call in there!"

Huxley walked back toward the kids. "Unfortunately, radio signals contain a lot of electronic noise or interference from radar antennas, radio stations, and many other sources," he said. "The only interference for optical SETI is lightning, which is only there during storms. This is where KISS comes in. The less complicated you make something, the less wasted thought and valuable time you have to put into it.

"Scientists have learned that a pulsed laser **accentuates** light, and can outshine many of the brightest stars in the sky," Huxley added, "making it the perfect choice for chasing after alien life out there in the cosmos. So, to answer your second question, Piper, all an alien needs to phone home is a small, handheld laser phone."

"That sounds cool," Piper said.

"Speaking of sounds, put these on," Huxley said, handing Peter and Piper black headsets with cushioned earphones. "Let's listen in and see if the aliens are talking to us today."

"Now, this is awesome," Peter said. "But how do we know that aliens aren't here on earth already?"

"We don't!" Dr. Huxley said, smiling. "We just don't know."

Rocky Road

Peter and his mom thanked Dr. Huxley for meeting with the kids.

Piper curtsied toward Huxley. "Thank you, sir, and I'll try my best to KISS in everything I do," she said. "But, in my case, I think it'll stand for Keep It Simple Smarty. I think that fits me better."

"I agree," Huxley laughed.

As they left the building, Peter said, "That was awesomely cool, Mom!"

"Yeah, really cool," Piper replied. "I bet kids in regular school don't get to go there and listen to alien space sounds."

"Mom, can I have one of those telescopes for Christmas?" Peter asked.

"We'll see, dear," Mom said.

Peter was about to say something else when he spotted Baldy heading their way. Who is this guy and how did he get away from the MPs and find us, Peter thought.

Peter had to get Baldy away from his mom and Piper. "Get Mom into the SUV. I'll be back soon," he whispered to Piper, then handed her his backpack and iPod.

"Mom, I've got to use the restroom. I'll be back in a few minutes. Okay?" Peter asked.

"Sure, but don't get lost. I want to go up to the Continental Divide before we pick up Breadloaf at the campground and get on the road," Mom said.

Baldy emerged from between two other SUVs off to Peter's right. Peter turned back toward the building. The man hesitated for a second and then followed. Instead of going into the building, Peter went around the side and began to run. He almost turned his ankle in one of several post-holes being dug for a fence around the building. He looked over his shoulder when he reached the end of the building. Baldy was just rounding the corner in a slow jog, but bolted into a dead run when he saw Peter.

Peter thought he might be able to lose him among the boulders and sneak back to Piper and his mom. He scrambled over three boulders before he looked back.

Baldy shouted, "Hey, kid get back here, I just want to talk to you."

Yeah, right, and I want to be a lion tamer without a whip or a chair, Peter thought.

Baldy was getting closer as they zigzagged up the boulders. The cutouts in the cliff reminded Peter of Siamese twins. He suddenly realized how stupid he had been. If something happened to him out here, no one would know. All he had done was make it easier for Baldy.

Peter cut to the left and slid to a stop. He was at the top of the boulders with a flat red wall in front and to the right of him. To his left, there was a ten-foot-deep ravine created by three large boulders butted up against each other. The closest of the three boulders was an eight-foot jump. Just do it, he thought.

Baldy suddenly appeared just below Peter. Peter noticed a gold ring with a large red ruby in its center on the man's right hand.

"I got you now, kid," Baldy said, breathing and sweating heavily.

Peter dashed to the boulder's edge. "Nikes don't fail me now!" he shouted.

Peter soared into the air and landed just beyond the ledge. When he turned around, he saw Baldy huffing and puffing at full speed toward the boulder.

Baldy jumped too soon and landed short of the boulder. He slid into the ravine and started screaming. Peter saw him stand up and brush himself off. He could tell that Baldy was okay.

Peter had to get back to the SUV, so he ignored Baldy's screaming. He turned to look for another way down when his legs slid out from under him. Peter landed on his bottom and slid down the boulder's smooth surface like a wild ride down a water slide.

A third of the way down, the smooth surface changed to gravely red dirt. The distant ground below Peter came into view. It was covered in softball-sized rocks and broken glass. Peter dug his right heel into the dirt, using it like a rudder, causing him to drift away from the rocks and glass. Suddenly, the boulder beneath him was gone.

Where am I?

Peter rolled head over heels down the rest of the hill, stopping when he made it to level ground. He laid there, feeling like a football player after the last post-season game. It didn't feel like he had broken anything. He was trying not to moan when he suddenly heard footsteps.

"What are you doing just lying here?" Piper said. "Mom's been wondering what's taking you so long."

Peter opened his eyes and saw that he was right behind the observatory building.

"And what did you do with your shoes?" Piper asked, picking up one shoe that was a few feet away from Peter. She waved it at him. "How come I can never leave you alone? You always seem to get lost. If someone had caught you going to the bathroom among these boulders, you would have really embarrassed Mom." She found the other shoe and tossed them both to Peter as he wearily sat up.

"Now, let's get going!" Piper commanded. "I'll tell Mom you're coming. And please knock some of that dirt off your clothes." She folded her arms and shook her head. "Boys!" she said, strutting off.

Peter scanned the boulders while dusting the dirt off his clothes. He should have been taken out of there in an ambulance. But everything felt okay. He was just a little sore from the fall, or was it the landing? He'd have to stop in the lobby to let them know somebody was stuck up in the boulders. *Then again, maybe he shouldn't tell anyone, he thought.*

Flying Tumbleweed

Peter and Piper sat in the back of the SUV as it rolled down Groom Lake Road in Nevada. Their mom was humming softly to a song on the radio. Peter stared at a satellite map of southeast Nevada that he had downloaded earlier. He curled his shoulders forward, stretching them to relieve the ache from his fall.

Even with all of their traveling, they had never been in the Southwest before. It was barren, just like the **arid** landscapes Peter had seen in old cowboy movies. And just like in the movies, the setting sun created a beautiful, reddish-purple glow on the horizon. Peter could almost imagine what it was like to be a Pony Express rider in the Old West delivering mail to small-town post offices in the area.

The airflow off the RV in front of them tossed tumbleweeds across the desert. Every now and then, one would fly into the air for just a few seconds. With the sun filtering through them, they looked like mini flying saucers spinning through the air, lights blinking on the edges.

"So?" Piper asked, breaking the silence in the back seat. "Are we going to see any flying saucers filled with aliens tonight, and is this Area 51 going to be as creepy as Hangar 18 was?"

Peter turned to his sister and bugged out his eyes, showing all the white on his eyeballs. "It'll be creepier, because that's where the aliens turn little girls into zombie slaves. And when they finally grow into women, the aliens..."

"Mom, Peter's trying to scare me again!" Piper shouted.

"...make them bake chocolate chip cookies because aliens love chocolate chip cookies," Peter finished.

"Okay, Peter, that's enough," Mom said. "How far am I supposed to go on this road and which way do I turn, Almighty Navigator?"

"We need to head southwest to Papoose Lake," Peter said. "But this road turns north and I don't see any roads heading southwest on this satellite map."

"I thought you said this road led to Area 51," Piper said.

"It does," Peter said, "but we want to go to Papoose Lake. I found an interview online with a physicist named Bob Lazar. He claims to have worked on alien spacecraft propulsion systems at an underground hangar near Papoose Lake back in the late 1980s."

"Hang on!" Mom screamed.

SCCRREEEECH!

The SUV squealed as it braked and swerved into a left turn. Peter would have slid into his sister if his seatbelt hadn't held him secure. The SUV's two right wheels lifted off the ground a few inches, and then slammed back to the dirt trail they had turned on. It was a good thing they had left Breadloaf at a campground or she would have rolled over for sure.

"Alright! Wasn't that fun?" Mom asked. "I think I found a road that should take us southwest. It's not paved, but that's okay; we haven't gone four-wheeling in a while."

"Mom, is this a smart thing to do?" Piper asked in a worried tone.

"Sure, honey," Mom said. "They wouldn't have put a road here if they didn't want us to use it. Besides, we'll just go 20 or 30 miles and see if there's anything worthwhile to look at."

Piper eyed Peter and shrugged.

"Okay, let us know if you see any little green men running around out here," Piper said.

Peter knew not to question his mom's logic. It was like hitting a brick wall going 100 miles an hour. The funny thing was that she almost always turned out to be right, which always baffled him.

KISS

The SUV bounced over the rugged terrain, as darkness settled over the desert. Peter turned back to his computer. He felt like they weren't solving the mystery. Sure, they had learned a lot, especially about SETI, but they were here to figure out who had sent the postcard, not to be driving around like tourists.

Peter was missing a piece of the puzzle, but he wasn't sure what it was. When he had misplaced or was missing something, his mom always told him to retrace his steps to find it. Maybe that's what he needed to do, start from the beginning. Peter pulled out the copy of the postcard to reread its message.

"What are you going to do with that?" Piper asked her brother.

"We're missing something," Peter said. "I'm hoping that by reading the postcard again, it'll help me figure out what it is we're missing."

Dear Alien,

... life here is lonely. I miss our home. ... on this planet ... funny ... people look at me green ... It has short ... and ... n ... cover ... skin ... guess ... scare them. Only ... understand. In ... take control of ... ... I must blend in ... the other ... at school, but I do not know how ... Meet me at the OSET IUFOMARC next Saturday night.

Your Yellow Alien

Peter scratched his head, patted his knee, and finally shook the postcard in frustration. "I don't know," he said. "Maybe I'm just not smart enough to figure this one out."

"That will be the day," Piper said. "You're the smartest kid I know. Besides, it sounds pretty simple to me. One alien is writing to another alien. It's as simple as that. Remember what Dr. Huxley said, KISS, Keep It Simple Stupid."

Peter scrutinized the message again. How could he look at it in a simpler way? He glanced out the SUV's window. Rays of light, created by the setting sun, danced throughout the billowy clouds at the top of a distant mountain range.

Peter began to notice the patterns the rays created in the darkening clouds. For a second he saw the shape of a dog, then a rhinoceros, and then a skull. That reminded him of that awesome picture Piper had shown him a few weeks before. It was a picture of a skull; at least until you squinted your eyes, then you could see a

picture of a young woman sitting at a vanity looking into the mirror.

As he thought about the skull, his eyes were drawn to the letter again. The missing piece of the puzzle was there. He could feel it.

It was begging to be found! But it was just out of his grasp.

Keep it simp—, he thought. Suddenly, he saw it.

The Missing Piece

"Thanks, sis." Peter said.

Piper eyed her brother suspiciously. "For what?" she asked.

"For helping me find the missing puzzle piece," Peter said.

"Okay!" Piper replied. "But, how did I do that?"

"The skull and young woman," Peter said.

"Okay," Piper said. "I take back what I said. Maybe you're not the smartest person I know. What are you talking about? Skull, young woman?"

"You know," Peter said. "That double image picture you showed me of the skull and young woman. Remembering it helped me to see what I have been missing.

"I've been going by what the message said, not by what it didn't say or what I couldn't read," Peter added. "The water-smeared words are the missing piece of the puzzle. Without them, the message sounds mysterious, but with them, it could be something very simple."

"Or something more complicated and bad," Piper suggested. "Like the aliens are planning an invasion where they take over the world by swaappinng thheirr braaiins inntoo ouur boodiies," Piper suggested, her voice vibrating as the SUV bounced over a series of bumps.

"It sounds like the aliens got to your brain first!" Peter said. "Since we don't know what the missing words are, we need to focus on the two complete sentences. "Life here is lonely" is clear with no smudges. That leaves "Meet me at the OSETIUFOMRC next Saturday night." It has two smudged water spots, one between the capital letters T and I, and one between the letters M and R."

Peter fumbled through his backpack and pulled out a magnifying glass. He looked at the letters closely. "Whoa! I didn't see this before."

"See what?" Piper asked.

"There's another T," Peter said. "It's faded from the water, but it's there. There's also a space between the second T and the I." He slid the magnifying glass over. "Uh oh! That changes everything."

"What changes everything?" Piper said, wanting to punch her brother in the arm for making her ask for answers.

"There's a small & between the M and R," Peter declared. "It's blurred, but I can see it pretty well with the magnifying glass."

Peter flung open his notebook and flipped to a page that had space for him to write on. He wrote OSETT IUFOM&RC. "I think we've been on a wild goose chase," he said, nodding his head up and down.

"Okay, this is the last time I'm going to ask," Piper said. "From now on give me your complete thoughts in sentences I can understand. Why have we been on a wild goose chase?"

Peter thrust his notebook at Piper. "There is no SETI or OSETI in this message which means that SETI has nothing to do with finding the message's writer. We just wasted our time going to see Dr. Huxley, although, it was pretty awesome."

Partners Forever

"Hold it," Piper said. "I have to do an essay on something that has nothing to do with the real meaning of this postcard. That's not fair. Besides, you're wrong."

"No, I'm not!" Peter said.

"Yes, you are!" Piper fired back.

"No, I'm–. Why am I wrong?" Peter asked, knowing he was going to regret having asked Piper that question.

Piper smiled. "You're wrong because if we hadn't visited Dr. Huxley, I would never have heard of KISS and I would not have reminded you about how you have to Keep It Simple Stupid," she said. "And if you hadn't kept it simple, you wouldn't have remembered the skull and young woman, and therefore, you wouldn't have figured it out. See, I'm smart, too!"

Peter had to smile. "Yes, you are," he said. "We make a great team."

"We sure do," Piper said. "And don't you ever forget it. Partners forever, right?" Piper reached out her hand.

"Pinky swear," Peter said, wrapping his little finger around hers.

Piper glanced at Peter's notebook. Below where Peter had written OSETT IUFOM&RC was Dr. Huxley's name, phone number, and address of the observatory.

A large smile broke out on Piper's face. "Peter, Dr. Huxley's observatory helped us out more than you think," she said.

"Really, how?" Peter asked.

Before Piper answered Peter, she noticed her mom had weaved their one-car caravan through a valley of low hills. She spotted a grove of trees up ahead.

"Mom, pull over by those trees," Piper said. "We don't need to go any further."

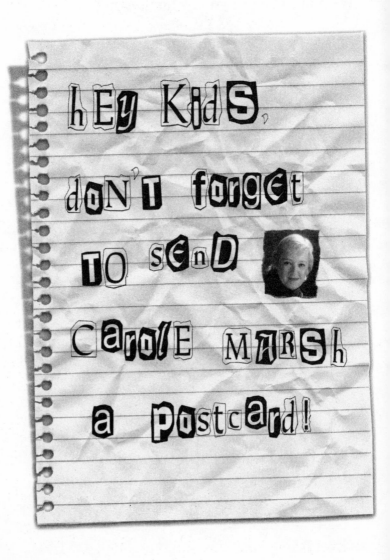

UFO Central

The Post family piled out of the SUV. Mom scanned the night sky above. It was a pitch-black canvas filled with more brilliant stars than she had seen since growing up on a farm in rural Pennsylvania. Unfortunately, there were a bunch of cumulus clouds to the north moving in their direction. Weird-looking lightning was pinging back and forth throughout the clouds.

"What does it stand for again?" Mom asked.

"We're not sure of the OSETT part yet," Peter said. "But the second acronym stands for International UFO Museum and Research Center. We think that it might be in Roswell, New Mexico, because that's 'UFO Central.' Everything and anything to do with UFOs is there. But I can research it more when we get back in range of a wireless Internet signal."

"So you're saying we won't find any UFOs here," Mom said.

"Well, that memo we found in Hangar 18's morgue seemed to say they were here," Peter said. "But that was a long time ago, so I doubt it."

As Mom and Piper gazed into the sky behind Peter, their eyes began to widen. "Peter, if there are no UFOs here, then what are those?" Piper said, pointing over her brother's shoulder.

Fireworks

Peter turned to look where Piper was pointing. There were large billowy clouds over where Area 51 should be, just about ten miles north of them. Multicolored lightning bolts—if that's what they were—crackled in the clouds without making a sound. It appeared to be high voltage charges leaping between clouds; the charges were mostly green, with small amounts of red and blue arcs mixed in.

Peter felt the electricity in the air particles surrounding him. He held his hands up in front of his face and watched tiny arcs flash back and forth between his fingers. Awesome, he thought. The clouds began to move. One cloud circled another, and then the circled cloud circled back.

Piper wrapped her arm through Peter's, but leaped back when they both received a mild shock from each other. "Peter, I don't like this," Piper said, her voice quivering. "Let's get out of here!"

"What are you talking about?" Peter said. "This is awesome!"

Mom stepped forward and put her hand on Peter's shoulder. "I think your sister's right, Peter. We need to leave."

"Aw, come on, Mom," Peter objected. "It's like watching Fourth of July fireworks."

As soon as Peter spoke, the clouds separated in a bright flash, like an explosion had sent them hurtling in all directions. Two of the clouds rocketed toward them, without a sound, at incredible speed. Bright-green, high-voltage charges flashed back and forth between the clouds. Red voltage charges danced brilliantly in an uncontrolled pattern around their outer edges. As they got closer, they became more streamlined, more saucer-looking. The saucer-shaped clouds kicked up dust and tumbleweeds as they barreled over the trees above Peter's head.

"AAAAAAHHHHHHH!" Piper began screaming, pointing out into the desert in front of them.

BBOOOOMMMMM!

An ear-splitting sonic boom tore through the sky, shaking the ground furiously, as a green mist fell over Peter, Piper, and their mother.

Piper screamed again and pulled at Peter's arm. Through the mist, heading toward them, a pair of green eyes appeared, then another, and another. Piper let go of her brother and ran back to the SUV, screaming all the way.

In a panic, Mom shouted. "Peter, let's go!"

With the clouds gone and Piper in the SUV, the desert grew quiet.

Peter kept his eyes on the pair of green eyes closest to him. He squatted down and picked up a thick, short stick at his feet. "Mom, don't run," he said. "Just back up slowly to the car." Peter lifted the stick behind his head, and flung it at the creature as soon as its outline appeared through the lingering mist.

"OWWWOOOO!" The coyote yelped. It turned and limped back into the desert, the rest of its pack following close behind.

Peter turned to his mom. "Are you okay?" he asked. "You look like you've seen a Martian or something."

"Very funny, Peter," Mom said.

Little Green Men

Peter climbed into the back seat of the SUV. "Now, *that* was awesome!" he shouted. "I can't wait to tell Dad about it." He glanced at Piper, who was sitting motionless with her hands in her lap. "You okay, sis?" he said, grinning. "You look like you've seen a—."

"Peter!" Mom interrupted, turning the SUV around and heading back to the main road.

Piper started to giggle. "Okay, okay, so I freaked out," she said. "I really thought we were being attacked by little green aliens with luminescent green eyes." She folded her arms over her chest. "There, does that make you feel better, Peter?"

"Sis," Peter said, "short of having a picture of you screaming and running to the car, I couldn't feel any better."

Piper stuck her tongue out at him. "Were those things UFOs?" Piper asked.

"To us they were definitely Unidentified Flying Objects!" Peter said. "But to the people up at Dreamland, they're probably some top secret project involving some new aircraft. That is where the U2 spy plane, the SR-71, and the stealth bomber were designed and put through all their flight tests. I'll bet that what we just saw was something similar. But, man, was that awesome or what?"

"Sooo, youu donn't thhink thaat theyy weere aalien spaacecrraft?" Piper asked, her voice vibrating again.

"Nah," Peter said. "When I watched those things zoom over, I could swear I saw a blue Air Force insignia on the bottom of one of them. So I'm sure the U.S. military designed them. But that doesn't mean we didn't get the technology from somewhere else.

"Who knows—maybe we got it from your little green men," Peter added with a wink.

Roswell

Mom stared at all the cars heading in the same direction as her SUV. They had left Breadloaf at a nearby campground and were lucky to get the last available RV site. All the campgrounds and hotels were sold out for Roswell's annual UFO Festival. Mom decided it would be the perfect windup to their trip, especially after that scary incident with the coyotes yesterday.

"Mom, how long is it before we get to town?" Piper whined.

"Ten more minutes," Mom said.

"That's what you always say," Piper replied.

"This time I mean it," Mom said. "Traffic's moving slow because of the festival activities.

I wonder how many of these people actually live in this small town."

Peter shut the laptop. "I just checked the festival's Internet site and the parade this evening starts in a little over an hour. There's a costume contest, too. The judging for the costume contest goes on during the parade and the winners are picked after the parade ends."

"Costume contest!" Mom said. "That sounds like fun."

"Peter, do you think the reason the alien chose to meet her alien friend today was because everyone would be running around in alien costumes, so no one would know they were real aliens?" Piper asked.

"Hmm!" Peter said. "I hadn't thought of that, but it's possible. If you want to hide something, what better place is there than right under people's noses. We'll have to keep our eyes wide open."

"Here we are," Mom sang out, turning a corner into Roswell's downtown area. The sun had set and the lampposts gave off an otherworldly green glow. All the storefront windows glowed brightly with neon green outlines. Mom decided green was going to be her least favorite color after this trip.

"We have to find the museum," Peter said. "I know it's located downtown."

"There it is!" Piper shouted. "Right over there. See the giant saucer on top of their sign? Peter, this isn't going to be easy; look at all the aliens walking around."

The museum was in an old movie theater a few doors down from a costume shop. Mannequins in brightly colored alien costumes posed in the shop windows. Next to the costume shop was the Alien Boutique Beauty Salon.

Mom had taken her curlers out before leaving the campground, but this was the perfect chance to get someone else to pamper her.

"You guys go in search of your alien," Mom said. "I'm going to get my hair done. Meet me out front of the museum in an hour. Okay?"

Peter and Piper jumped out of the car and headed through the crowd toward the museum.

"Okay," Peter shouted.

Blue Baldy

Peter wriggled his way through the crowd of aliens with Piper stuck like glue behind him. The costumes look so real, Piper thought. The front doors to the museum had been propped open. Peter and Piper slipped in unnoticed by all the aliens in attendance.

"Peter, how are we ever going to find our alien?" Piper asked. "I can't even tell if some of these aliens are men or women, boys or girls."

"I know what you mean," Peter said. "I think we're looking for a young female alien, but I don't know how to find her."

"Kai gatk sitap somla pah fopi," someone said behind Peter.

Peter and Piper turned to find a tall, blue-headed alien speaking to them. His head looked like an upside-down fishbowl with big, round, bug-looking eyes, no nose, and a very tiny mouth. He had on long, silvery, flowing robes. He lifted his right hand toward Peter and spread his fingers into a V, giving the Vulcan salute. A gold ring with a ruby in the center rested on the alien's middle finger.

"I got you now, kid," the alien said.

Peter grabbed Piper's hand. "Come on!" he shouted, and dragged her out the museum door. He turned to the right and bobbed and weaved his way through the sea of aliens. He ran down an alley and yanked Piper to the ground behind a huge garbage container. Piper stared at a picture of an ugly, mean-looking alien on a post next to them. Above the picture it said:

A door across the alley opened and two aliens wandered out. "Okay," the first one said in a male voice. "Meet me at the outside entrance to the museum in about 20 minutes." The other alien nodded and they walked away in separate directions.

That's it, Peter thought. OSETT was shorthand for "outside entrance to the," so they had to look for their alien outside of the museum, not inside.

"Come on, let's go," Peter said.

"But what if the bad alien's not gone yet," Piper said. "He could be trying to capture us and take us back to his home planet, or maybe he wants to suck our brains..."

"Piper, he's not an alien," Peter said. "That's the bald guy who chased us in the hangar back in Dayton. He's the same one who was chasing me up in the boulders behind the observatory."

"So that's why you were up in the boulders," Piper said. "Oh! I thought you were...ahh, never mind."

"Why does this guy keep chasing us?" Peter asked himself. Next to the garbage bin was a gallon container of used vegetable oil. Peter grabbed it. "Let's go! We'll circle the block and see if he's anywhere around. If not, we'll go back to the museum."

Peter and Piper tiptoed down the alley and peeked around the corner. No one was there. Everyone was in front of the museum where the parade was about to get underway. They walked past a community recreation center and a beautiful pool filled with crystal blue water. They got to the next corner and peeked around it. There he was!

Splash!

Baldy was heading toward the kids. Occasionally, he would jump up to peer over the alien hordes as he tried to find them.

Peter turned to his sister. "We're going to end this right now, come on," he said. He turned around and headed back to the pool.

A few minutes later, Baldy came around the corner. Peter put his thumb and forefinger in his mouth and whistled loudly. Baldy came running toward them, his big blue head bobbling side to side on his shoulders. He slowed to a jog as he approached them and then came to a stop.

"Okay, kid," Baldy called out, panting for breath. "This is the end of the trail." He took a step toward Peter. "I'm going to have a talk with your fath–." Baldy was so focused on Peter and

Piper that he hadn't looked at the ground in front of him. He stepped onto the plastic lining covering the cement around the pool. Peter had coated it in oil.

Baldy's arms flew into the air as his feet did an Irish jig trying to keep him upright. That only lasted a few seconds. As he fell flat on his back, his forward motion carried him the last few feet to the pool's edge.

SPLASH! Baldy slid over the side. His big blue head popped off and bobbed freely in the water as he thrashed about.

Peter looked at his James Bond watch. "Come on," he said. "The parade starts in five minutes." He and Piper ran around the edge of the oil slick and back to the front of the museum, but they couldn't see their mom anywhere.

Oh! I'm Sorry

"Where have you guys been?" Mom asked.

Peter and Piper turned toward their mother's voice. A couple of aliens stood a few feet away. One alien was covered in shimmering green scales. Along with her face and neck, her hair was green and slicked back flat on her head. She had gigantic, bright red lips and big white eyes with tiny black pupils and no eyebrows. A long, black, shimmering cape hung down her back.

Piper jumped. "Oh my gosh, Mom, is that you?"

"Yes, dear," Mom said, spinning around like a model. "How do I look?"

"Like an alien mom, from some fish-like planet," Piper replied.

"Perfect!" Mom said. "That's the look I was going for."

Another alien standing next to her wore black and brown robes and a cheap Star Wars character mask. "How about me?" he asked.

"Dad!" Both Peter and Piper screamed. They ran to their father and hugged him.

"Dad, how did you get here?" Peter asked.

"Mom called me last night and told me you were going to be here," Dad said. "So I thought I'd fly down just for the weekend. I would have had a better costume, but I didn't know about the parade until I got here."

Just then, a very soggy bald man walked up behind Peter. He held a large blue head under his arm like a football helmet.

Piper saw the man coming and moved behind her father.

"John, how on earth did you get all wet?" Dad asked Baldy.

"It's a long story," John replied.

Peter turned to see Baldy standing behind him. "Uhh!" Peter said. "You know this guy, Dad?"

"Of course," Dad said. "John's a retired postal policeman and a good friend of mine."

"Paul, you didn't?" Mom said.

"Okay, okay," Dad said. "So I'm a worrywart. I had John shadowing you around the country to make sure you didn't run into any trouble. He was supposed to call me if you did."

"How on earth did you keep track of us?" Mom asked John.

John nodded toward Paul.

"I...ahh..." Dad stammered. "I put a tracking bug inside Breadloaf."

"You didn't!" Mom said.

"That's awesome, Dad!" Peter said.

"Listen, Paul," John said. "I'm going to head home. I can tell you for sure that your son has everything under control. You have nothing to be worried about. He can take care of the three of them." He winked at Peter. "You guys have a good trip," John said, shaking Paul's hand. He glared at Peter for a second, and then put his hand out.

Peter shook it. "I'm sorry, I didn't know."

"No problem," John said with a smile. "I needed the exercise, and a good swim never hurt anyone. Truce?"

"Truce," Peter replied.

Mission Accomplished

Peter and Piper waved at their parents. "We'll meet you at the judges' stand," Peter said to his mom and dad as they joined the parade.

Peter looked around. All the aliens were gone. There was only a dark-skinned young girl standing outside the museum with them. They had missed their chance at finding the alien. Oh well, he thought. You can't win them all.

"I guess we'll never find out if the alien showed up here or not," Piper said.

The young girl walked over to them. "Excuse me," she said. "I got here a little late. Have you seen another girl, who looks like me, around here? She is my cousin and I cannot find her. I told her I would meet her at the outside entrance to the museum."

Peter and Piper looked at each other with big smiles.

"No way!" Peter said.

Piper jumped up and down shouting, "We did it! We did it!" Piper suddenly stopped jumping. "Hold it," Piper said. "Did you send your cousin a postcard?"

"Yes, how did you know?" the girl replied.

"I can't believe it!" Peter said. "We thought we'd never find you. Your cousin never received your postcard. It ended up in the dead letter file at our dad's post office in Pennsylvania. The addresses were all smeared and they couldn't deliver it. We've been using it to try to find you."

"You have been looking for me? Why?" the girl asked.

"We thought you were an alien from a galaxy far, far away who was going to suck out our brains and make us into mindless zombie slaves," Piper said. "But you don't look like an alien. You don't even look like all the fake aliens here."

"I am an alien," the girl replied. "I am just not the kind you are thinking of. I was born in Venezuela, in South America. My dad works for a large oil company and we came here a year ago with his company. My name is Maria Sanchez."

Peter laughed.

"What is so funny?" Maria asked.

"Well, it's kind of a long story," Peter said. "But it starts with your postcard leading us to think you were an alien from outer space." Peter yanked the copy of the postcard out of his pocket and gave it to Maria. He watched as she read it. She started to laugh.

"My, this sounds so, so...what is the word...omi," Maria said.

"Ominous," Peter finished.

"Yes, ominous," Maria repeated.

"Why do you call each other alien?" Piper asked. "And do you remember what you wrote?"

"My cousin moved to New York a month before we moved to New Mexico," Maria replied. "We call each other alien, because your country is very different from ours and we feel like we are visitors from another planet."

Maria looked at the copy of the postcard. "I remember what I wrote," she said, pausing for a second:

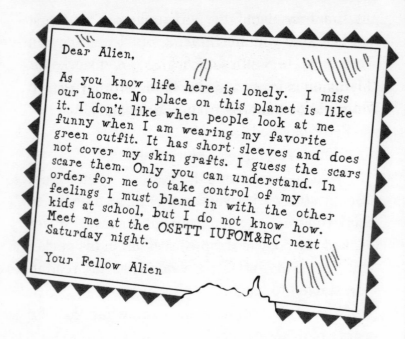

Dear Alien,

As you know life here is lonely. I miss our home. No place on this planet is like it. I don't like when people look at me funny when I am wearing my favorite green outfit. It has short sleeves and does not cover my skin grafts. I guess the scars scare them. Only you can understand. In order for me to take control of my feelings I must blend in with the other kids at school, but I do not know how. Meet me at the OSETT IUFOM&RC next Saturday night.

Your Fellow Alien

"OSETT stands for, Outside–." Maria started.

"Outside entrance to the," Peter interrupted.

"Yes," Maria said. "I so wanted to see my cousin because, as I said, I am very lonely. It has been hard for me to make friends." Maria held out both of her arms to show her scars.

"My cousin and I were playing near a fire when we were six years old," Maria said. "Our clothes caught on fire. By the time our fathers put the flames out, both of my arms and my cousin's legs were burned."

"Maria," Piper said, sticking out her hand. "My name is Piper and this is my brother Peter. We would be honored to be your friends."

Second Place

Mom sat at the outdoor café with Paul, Peter, Piper, and Maria. Her second place trophy, for most creative costume, sat on the ground next to her. She listened as Peter recalled their adventures for his dad and Maria.

"I threw a big stick at the coyotes and they took off running," Peter said.

"No way!" Dad said, thinking Peter was exaggerating his story just a little. "You guys are lucky you didn't get caught," he winked at Mom. "From what I hear, they have a lot of top-secret stuff going on at Area 51."

"You are kind of quiet, Piper," Maria asked. "How come?"

"I don't know," Piper said. "I guess I was really hoping you were an alien from outer space.

I'm happy you're not, but wouldn't it be cool to meet someone from another planet?"

"Yeah," Peter said. He had slipped on an alien mask. "Then they could help me suck out your brains and turn you and Maria into mindless zombie slaves." Peter chased his sister and Maria around the park. They waved their hands in the air, running and yelling at the top of their lungs, "Someone save us, don't let the ugly alien take our brains!"

Peter and Piper stopped when they noticed an adult female alien walk up to their parents with a tray of cookies in her webbed hands.

"Would you like some chocolate chip cookies?" she asked.

The two siblings looked at each other and burst out laughing.

THE END

Hey Kids,
Send Carole Marsh a postcard—
get a postcard from me!

Postlogue

Peter and Piper stuffed their gear into the SUV. Piper took the card with Maria's address out of her pocket and stuck it into her pink fanny pack.

"Can you guys go let the office know we're leaving and sign us out?" Mom asked. "I'll finish packing the SUV."

"Sure, Mom," Peter said. "We'll take care of it."

"Hey Piper," Peter said. "On our way back through Dayton, we should stop at Wright-Patterson and see if we can find those missing aliens."

Piper glared at him. "Once is enough, thank you!" she replied.

As Peter and Piper walked away, a storage bin door on the side of Breadloaf opened slowly. Two green eyes peered out cautiously, looking around the campground.

Quietly, a little green man slid down to the ground. A Chicago Cubs baseball cap covered his huge head. His bulging eyes poked out from beneath the cap's rim.

"No way I am going there," the little green man mumbled. "Area 51 was boring enough. There's *got to be something more exciting on this planet. I must phone home."*

The alien wore a shimmering, skin-tight, light blue jump suit and a pair of silver sneakers with little rockets on each side. Binoculars hung around his scrawny neck, and a camera bag was slung over his slender shoulder. He plucked a small device from the black belt around his tiny waist. He stuck the device into a hole on the side of his head and pressed a button on his belt.

"Hi Mom, it's me," the little green man said.

As he talked, he pressed another small silver button on his belt. The rockets on his sneakers powered up silently and an invisible stream of pure energy suddenly catapulted him into the sky.

Piper turned quickly. She could have sworn she'd seen an alien out of the corner of her eye. But there was nothing there.

Maybe someday, Piper thought, someday.

About the
Author

Carole Marsh is an author and publisher who has written many works of fiction and non-fiction for young readers. She travels throughout the United States and around the world to research her books. In 1979, Carole Marsh was named Communicator of the Year for her corporate communications work with major national and international corporations.

Marsh is the founder and CEO of Gallopade International, established in 1979. Today, Gallopade International is widely recognized as a leading source of educational materials for every state and many countries. Marsh and Gallopade were recipients of the 2004 Teachers' Choice Award. Marsh has written more than 50 Carole Marsh Mysteries™. In 2007, she was named Georgia Author of the Year. Years ago, her children, Michele and Michael, were the original characters in her mystery books. Today, they continue the Carole Marsh Books tradition by working at Gallopade. By adding grandchildren Grant and Christina as new mystery characters, she has continued the tradition for a third generation.

Ms. Marsh welcomes correspondence from her readers. You can e-mail her at fanclub@gallopade.com, visit the carolemarshmysteries.com website, or write to her in care of Gallopade International, P.O. Box 2779, Peachtree City, Georgia, 30269 USA.

Talk About It!

1. Have you ever taken a road trip? If so, what was fun about it? If not, where would you like to go?

2. Do you believe in aliens? Why or why not?

3. If you were a spy with a special spy kit, what would you keep in it?

4. If you could talk to aliens, what would you ask them? What would you share with them about yourself and Earth?

5. Aliens can have some really cool names. What would your alien name be if you were an alien?

6. Can you think of any times you've felt like a visitor on a strange planet like Maria and her cousin do? When and why did you feel this way?

7. What do you think life would be like on an alien planet?

8. Why did Maria's scars make it harder for her to make friends?

Built-In Book Club

Bring it to Life!

1. What do you think aliens look like? Draw a portrait of your imagined alien.

2. Write a message to a friend and leave out certain words. Let your friend try to decipher your message by filling in the blanks!

3. Pretend you're an alien with your own language. In a small group, make up your own communication system. You can make up words, draw pictures, make up a sign language, etc. Then, share your new language with the other alien groups!

4. Imagine you're on vacation on another planet. Write a postcard to send to a friend on Earth.

5. You don't have to go to Roswell to have an Alien Parade! You can have your own! Get dressed up with your friends as wacky aliens. Then, go visit other friends or classrooms and show off your fantastic alien costumes!

6. Do you like Jell-O? It's not quite solid, but not quite liquid. It sure seems like something from another planet! Make green Jell-O and accompany it with some green apple juice (just add food coloring to the juice), and have yourself an out-of-this-world snack break.

Write six pen pal postcards. Write three to a Little Green Man (or girl!)...and then answer them!

Amazing Alien Trivia

1. In rural areas where there are fields of crops like corn, some mysterious patterns have appeared in the corn. These patterns are called crop circles. Since no one has been able to explain what causes these intricate patterns, some people think they are the artwork of aliens!

• Crop circles have been found in over 70 countries around the world!

• Farmers have claimed that their tools stop working in the middle of a crop circle!

2. If your job is to study aliens, you are an astrobiologist, or you could call yourself an exobiologist or a xenobiologist.

3. Life cannot be sustained without water, so scientists are always very excited when traces of water are found on other planets. This means that life might exist! For example, Europa, one of Jupiter's moons, is believed to have a layer of water under its surface. Astrobiologists have been taking a very close look at this moon.

4. In 1947 in Roswell, New Mexico, pieces of metal mysteriously came crashing out of the sky. Some people believed that they were pieces of a flying saucer flown by aliens!

5. People also claimed to have seen alien bodies in Roswell around the time of the falling metal. It was later discovered that the U.S. Air Force had been running tests at that time. The "aliens" were probably dummies used by the military for their tests.

6. Since 1996, an alien festival is held in Roswell every year, complete with a museum and Alien Masquerade Ball!

7. A man named Kenneth Arnold reported the first UFO sighting in 1947 at Mount Rainier, Washington. He claimed to have seen a series of nine flying, saucer-shaped objects of unusual size and speed. Arnold's initial description of the UFOs started the phrase "flying saucers."

Glossary

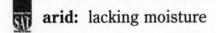 **accentuate:** to stress or emphasize

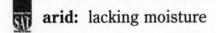 **arid:** lacking moisture

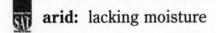 **camaraderie:** good will and lighthearted rapport between or among friends

envelop: to cover on all sides

 foil (v.): to prevent from being successful

forensic: related to courts or legal matters

galaxy: a very large group of stars; the earth and the sun are part of the Milky Way galaxy

morgue: a place where dead bodies are kept until identified or until arrangements for burial have been made

observatory: a building with telescopes and other equipment in it for studying the sun, moon, stars, planets, and weather

optical: related to the sense of sight; or designed to give help in seeing

paraphernalia: the articles or equipment used in a given activity

 perplex: to confuse or puzzle

propulsion: the process of propelling, or driving forward

The two "alien" cousins in this mystery kept in touch by being pen pals. Do you have a pen pal? It can be a lot of fun, and you can learn a lot, too!

Why you might like to be a pen pal:

1. Make a new friend. You might even be friends for life!

2. Improve your writing and reading skills.

3. Learn how people live in another town, state, or country.

4. Share thoughts and ideas with someone your own age.

5. Look forward to getting the mail every day—there might be something for you!

Pop Quiz

1. What is formaldehyde?

2. Who found the alien postcard in the Dead Letters Only box?

3. What does KISS stand for? Write it out in words.

4. What does Peter and Piper's father do for a living?

5. What name did Peter give to the family's RV?

6. What image helped Peter to discover the missing piece of the postcard?

7. To what or whom did the green eyes belong that the family saw in the desert?

8. What is John's nickname in the story?

TECH CONNECTS!

Hey, Kids!
Visit <u>www.carolemarshmysteries.com</u> to:

• Join the Carole Marsh Mysteries Fan Club!

• Learn some Amazing Alien Trivia!

• Learn more about Area 51!

• Download an Alien Word Search!

• Tackle an Alien Pop Quiz!

• Download a Scavenger Hunt!

• Make your own Alien!